For Annie Pearl Avery, a civil rights activist and foot soldier who courageously participated in the voting rights marches described in this book and is still walking the walk, volunteering her time to provide me and others with priceless guidance through the National Voting Rights Museum and Institute in Selma, Alabama —J.W.

Thank you, God, for the gifts. Dedicated to my grandmothers for climbing the hill to get us all to freedom. —S.W.E.

Visit us on the Web! randomhousekids.com

Educators and librarians, for a variety of teaching tools, visit us at RHTeachersLibrarians.com

Library of Congress Cataloging-in-Publication Data
Winter, Jonah.
Lillian's right to vote : a celebration of the Voting Rights Act of 1965 / Jonah Winter ; illustrator Shane Evans. —
First edition.
pages cm.
Summary: As an elderly woman, Lillian recalls that her great-great-grandparents were sold as slaves in front of a courthouse where only rich white men were allowed to vote, then the long fight that led to her right—and determination—to cast her ballot since the Voting Rights Act gave every American the right to vote.
ISBN 978-0-385-39028-6 (alk. paper) — ISBN 978-0-385-39029-3 (glb : alk. paper)
ISBN 978-0-385-39030-9 (ebk)
[1. Voting—Fiction. 2. African Americans—History—Fiction.] I. Evans, Shane, illustrator. II. Title.
PZ7.W75477Lil 2015
[E]—dc23
2014010937

The text of this book is set in Berling.
The illustrations were rendered in mixed media.

MANUFACTURED IN CHINA
10 9 8 7 6 5 4 3 2 1
First Edition

A CELEBRATION OF THE VOTING RIGHTS ACT OF 1965

LILLIAN'S RIGHT TO VOTE

BY

jonah winter

ILLUSTRATED BY

shane w. evans

schwartz & wade books · new york

A very old woman stands at the bottom of a very steep hill. It's Voting Day, she's an American, and by God, she is going to vote. Lillian is her name.

It's a long haul up that steep hill. It's a long haul when you've been alive for a hundred years. It's a long haul when you've lived the life that Lillian has—and walked so far in her shoes. When Lillian looks up, it's more than blue sky she sees. She sees history.

Lillian sees her great-great-grandparents Elijah and Sarah. They are standing side by side on an auction block. Sarah is holding their baby, Edmund. They are being sold as slaves in front of the very same Alabama courthouse where rich white men, and no one else, are allowed to vote.

Lillian starts her slow climb.

Though the sun shines brightly, Lillian sees a dark time from years long past. She sees her great-grandpa Edmund, now grown. He is owned by another man, forced to pick cotton from daybreak to nightfall—right here in this country where it is written that "all men are created equal." He sure doesn't have the right to vote. In fact, he doesn't have the right to do much at all—until after the Civil War, which will end slavery.

As Lillian inches up the hill, past one neighbor's house and then the next, she sees her great-grandpa Edmund on his way to vote for the first time—thanks to a law that was passed in 1870. The law is the Fifteenth Amendment to the US Constitution, which says that American citizens' right to vote "shall not be denied or abridged . . . on account of race, color, or previous condition of servitude." Even though the law does not allow women to vote, Great-Grandma Ida is with her husband. Lillian feels their dignity, and their pride, as they enter that courthouse for the first time.

But as Lillian continues, and the hill gets steeper—my, but that hill is steep—she sees what happens just twenty years later: right here in Alabama, there's her grandpa Isaac at the courthouse, being charged a poll tax to vote—a tax he doesn't have the money to pay. So much for that Fifteenth Amendment. So much for Grandpa Isaac's right to vote.

Lillian pauses to catch her breath, hearing now the voice of her uncle Levi. He is telling about those "tests" that he was forced to take when he tried to vote, and about the sneer on the registrar's face when he asked, "How many bubbles are in a bar of soap?" Her uncle's lips go tight as he recalls being asked to "name all sixty-seven judges in the state of Alabama"—and being turned away when he failed to answer such questions.

As Lillian pushes on, struggling to keep her balance, she sees a brave girl standing next to her mother and father as they try to register to vote. The year is 1920, and the Nineteenth Amendment has just passed, a law allowing women to vote. The girl is Lillian herself, with her mama and papa. They are being chased away by an angry mob. There's Mr. Bentley, the barber—and Mr. McCrory, who owns the ice cream shop. She feels the firm grip of her mother's hand as they run through the streets back home.

And though today the birds are singing and people are smiling, Lillian sees in vivid orange and brilliant red . . . the cross burning on the lawn of her girlhood home, set aflame by the same angry mob, just because her parents want to vote. This is something she will always see.

Lillian stops in her tracks, unable to keep going. As she stands there, she sees herself trying to register to vote for the very first time. She sees the blank piece of paper on which she must write down a section of the US Constitution, word for word, as it is being mumbled by the registrar— a test she could not pass. No one could.

"Are you going to vote?" she asks a young man who
passes her on her route.

"Yes, ma'am," he answers.

"You better," she says, and she means it.

For Lillian sees the funeral procession for a man named Jimmie Lee Jackson, a twenty-six-year-old shot by a policeman over nothing more than taking part in a peaceful protest. It is March 1965. All he'd wanted was justice—and the right to vote.

Looking up to the top of the hill, Lillian wonders how she'll ever make it. It looks so far, and she's so tired.

Though her feet and legs ache with one hundred years of walking, what fuels her ancient body is seeing those six hundred people beginning a peaceful protest march from Selma to Montgomery—people who, though they don't know it yet, will be stopped on a bridge in Selma by policemen with clubs. All they want is justice—and the right to vote. At the front is future congressman John Lewis, whose forehead will always bear the scar from where he was beaten.

As long as Lillian still has a pulse, she is going to vote—and so she keeps on climbing, keeps on seeing, this time the second march from Selma. This march also ends on the bridge, in a prayer led by the Reverend Martin Luther King Jr., whose dreams of justice for African Americans are already famous. Wherever he went, he lifted people up with his words—and his words still lift up Lillian, who, seeing the top of the hill, is not about to stop. Footstep by footstep, she keeps on going,

just as the marchers from Selma to Montgomery keep on going through the cold and rain, finally making it all the way to Montgomery on their third march. She sees them all—Martin Luther King, John Lewis, rabbis, priests, and 25,000 others. Lillian is there. She can still hear Reverend King asking how long they would have to wait for justice. She can still feel the power of his voice when he says "Not long."

And as she takes those final steps to the top of the hill, Lillian can still see how Reverend King was right. For she can hear the voice of President Lyndon Johnson on her TV, saying to America: *"Every American citizen must have an equal right to vote. . . . There is no duty which weighs more heavily on us than the duty we have to ensure that right. . . . All of us . . . must overcome the crippling legacy of bigotry and injustice. And we shall overcome."*

Before Lillian walks through the doors of the building, where you better believe she will vote, she looks up and sees the same blue sky—brighter than any sky she's ever seen—that she saw on August 6, 1965. That was the day President Johnson signed the Voting Rights Act: the one law protecting all Americans' RIGHT TO VOTE, in every state and every town, the one law protecting Lillian as a full-fledged citizen of the United States.

She enters the building. And as Lillian steps into the voting booth, once again, she sees herself stepping into the voting booth in 1965 for the very first time.

And she knows full well she would not be standing here today were it not for the people who marched . . . and the people who died . . . for her right to vote. Lillian touches her finger to the lever. And because she is a citizen of the United States of America, protected by the Voting Rights Act of 1965,

Lillian pushes that lever. Lillian votes.

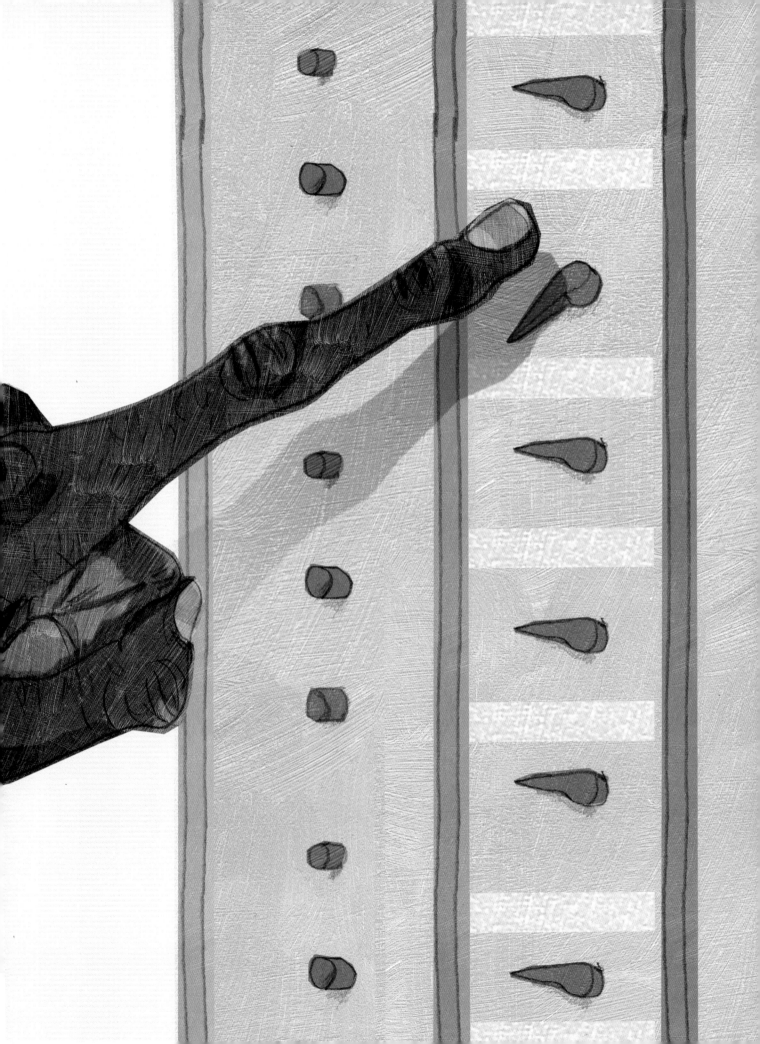

AUTHOR'S NOTE

When the United States of America was brand-new, back in the late 1700s, hardly any Americans had the right to vote. Generally, the only citizens who were allowed to cast their ballots were white men who owned property. Women, African Americans, Native Americans, and poor white men were excluded from the most important expression of democracy and equality. And though many changes were made to voting laws through the course of American history, women did not win the right to vote until 1920, and African Americans' right to vote was not protected by federal law until 1965.

      This book is intended as a commemoration of the fiftieth anniversary of that monumental piece of legislation, the Voting Rights Act of 1965. The act made it illegal for states to use literacy tests or poll taxes (or anything else) as a means of denying American citizens their right to vote. It also provided federal oversight of the election processes in the Southern states, where African Americans had historically been denied that right most often. The Voting Rights Act was passed only through the enormous courage and sacrifice of those who marched and protested—costing some their lives. Democratic president Lyndon B. Johnson's strong support of this legislation lost him a huge amount of popularity in the South among white voters, many of whom left the Democratic Party for the Republican Party.

My "Lillian" was inspired by Lillian Allen, a resident of Pittsburgh's Hill District, who was born in Alabama in 1908, the granddaughter of a slave. In 2008, at age one hundred, not only did she vote for the first African American president, Barack Obama, she also campaigned door to door in her hilly neighborhood, encouraging others much younger than her to vote. The image of this aged woman walking up a hill to vote seemed a fitting metaphor for the uphill climb faced by African Americans in the struggle for voting rights.

The sad coda to this story is that in 2013, the Supreme Court struck down a key provision of the Voting Rights Act of 1965, eliminating federal oversight of states' election processes. Since that decision, many states have created "voter ID laws," which require all citizens to present a state-issued photo ID when voting. Because such identification is often difficult for the poor and the elderly to obtain, these laws have the effect of denying many Americans a basic right—a right for which so many courageous people fought and died. The right to vote still needs protection. Will a new generation rise and continue this fight?